OWned
NAOMI

The Sleepover Club

Have you been invited to all these sleepovers?

The Sleepover Club
on the Farm

by Sue Mongredien

An imprint of HarperCollins*Publishers*

The Sleepover Club ® is a
registered trademark of HarperCollins*Publishers* Ltd

First published in Great Britain by Collins in 2001
Collins is an imprint of HarperCollins*Publishers* Ltd
77-85 Fulham Palace Road, Hammersmith,
London, W6 8JB

The HarperCollins website address is
www.**fire**and**water**.com

1 3 5 7 9 8 6 4 2

ISBN 0 00711771 X

The author asserts the moral right to
be identified as the author of the work.

Printed and bound in Great Britain by
Omnia Books Limited
Glasgow G64

Sleepover Kit List

1. Sleeping bag
2. Pillow
3. Pyjamas or a nightdress
4. Slippers
5. Toothbrush, toothpaste, soap etc
6. Towel
7. Teddy
8. A creepy story
9. Food for a midnight feast:
   chocolate, crisps, sweets, biscuits.
   In fact anything you like to eat.
10. Torch
11. Hairbrush
12. Hair things like a bobble or hairband,
    if you need them
13. Clean knickers and socks
14. Change of clothes for the next day
15. Sleepover diary and membership card

CHAPTER ONE

Baa! It's Lyndsey Lamb here. No, don't worry, you haven't picked up one of those books about talking animals by mistake. It's me, Lyndz from the Sleepover Club, really. I'm normally plain old Lyndz Collins, but ever since us Sleepover girls hung out on Mr Mackintosh's farm, the others have been calling me Lyndsey Lamb or Lambkin. And if Kenny's being horrible, she'll call me Lamb Chop!

Still, I'm not the only one to have got a silly new name. Uh-uh. Meet the rest of the club – that's Kenny Cow, Rosie Ram, Frankie Frog and

Flissy Foal! Us five are best mates and do everything together – well, most of the time anyway. More about THAT later...

I've just got a bit of time before my riding lesson to tell you all about our farm adventures. D'you know, until we went there, I'd always dreamed of being a famous jockey when I grow up, or running my own stables, or working in an animal rescue centre. But guess what I want to do now? Yep – live on a farm! I think it would be awesome being with so many animals all day, every day. Wouldn't it be fantastic?

But that's me. I absolutely LURVE animals. All of them – big, small, furry, woolly, wild, tame, claws, paws, hooves, whatever. Do you know what? I even think Kenny's pet rat Merlin is cute, which is a bit unusual. Me and Kenny seem to be the only two people in the world who aren't scared of him!

Not everyone's like that, though. If you asked Fliss if she'd like to live on a farm, she'd shudder and say, "No way!" She has dreams of living in a house like Posh and Becks when she's older – preferably when she's married to Ryan Scott from school! In fact, I reckon Fliss would actually like to *be* the next Posh Spice so she could buy as many clothes as she wants to. Now that's HER idea of heaven. Funny, isn't it, how different people are?

Lucky for me that the rest of the Sleepover Club were mad keen on the idea of a farm sleepover too, or we might never have got there. Frankie and Kenny love doing anything that's a bit out of the ordinary, and Rosie is always up for a bit of fun, so once I'd got those three on my side, that was that. No stopping us!

Anyway, let me begin at the beginning, as Mrs Weaver, our teacher, always says. It all started when we were having a sleepover at my house one Friday night. We were in my bedroom playing a game of Cat's Got The Measles when Mum shouted up the stairs that it was tea.

"Result!" Kenny cheered, rushing for the door. "I am sooo Hank Marvin."

"Who's he?" Fliss wanted to know. She was looking very puzzled.

"Hank Marvin – starving, geddit?" Kenny replied. "It's rhyming slang, isn't it?"

Fliss didn't look convinced. "Is it?" she asked.

"'Course it is," Kenny answered. "Honestly, Fliss, don't you ever watch *EastEnders*?"

"Yes, but..." Fliss was still frowning. "You're weird, Kenny. Didn't anyone ever tell you that?"

Downstairs, Mum was dishing up bangers, mash and beans. Everyone was already sitting around the table except my big brother Stuart. He was late home from school again, and boy, did Mum look cross about it.

"Where's that son of mine got to?" she grumbled, putting his plate in the oven to keep warm. "I told him to phone me if he was going to be late."

"He's probably stopped off at the farm, lucky thing," I said, spearing a sausage and biting the end off. Yum!

"Lyndz, cut your food up properly," Mum said at once. She's got a biiiiig thing about table manners, my mum. She says it's like feeding time at the zoo when our family sits down to eat. "Anyway, he still should have phoned me. He knows I only worry when he doesn't."

Stuart is still at school but works on Mr Mackintosh's farm down the road in his spare time. He's like me, he loves animals and wants to be a farmer when he's older. Awesome! I hope he does. It'll mean I'll be visiting him – and his animals, of course – ALL the time!

I'd been nagging him for absolutely ages to let me visit the farm with him because lambing season was about to start and I was dying to see some baby lambs. Soooo cute! Aren't baby animals simply THE most adorable things in the world? But even though I kept going on at him, Stu kept on putting me off, saying they were too busy at the farm to let little girls mess around. Little girls, indeed! Sometimes I hate boys.

Anyway, so we were just getting stuck into our tea when we heard a key turn in the front door. It was Stuart – at last.

"Nice of you to join us," my dad muttered

sarcastically as Stu came in, his face all pink from the cold.

"Why didn't you phone?" Mum said, rushing to get his plate out of the oven. "Here – sit down. Your tea's still warm."

"Thanks, Mum," he said, taking his coat off and sitting down. "I did try and phone you but the line was engaged for ages."

I went bright red then. Oops! That had been me. I'd phoned up this horoscope line to get the Sleepover Club horoscopes for the week, only the call seemed to last forever and ever. All five of us have got different star signs, you see, so I had to listen to all of them, didn't I?

"Sorry I'm late. I got chatting to Mrs Mack, up at the farm," he went on. "I just dropped in to say hello but ended up helping her out for a bit. Bad news – one of the ewes is really ill and has had her lambs early. They're tiny – and because the ewe is so ill, she can't feed them."

"Ahhhhh!" I said, biting my lip in concern. "Poor little lamby babies!"

"Poor poor lamby-wammies," Kenny said, teasing me.

"The teeny tiny little wittle baby lambykins have a poorly mummy!" Frankie added, with a grin.

I was about to get all indignant, but Stuart spoke before I could think of a crushing reply. "Actually, Lyndz, Mrs Mack was asking about you," he said. "Asking if you were very busy tomorrow."

"No, not really," I said in surprise. "Just a riding lesson. Why?"

"Well, she was wondering if you might like to help out with the – what was it? – the poor little wittle baby lambykins," he said. "She'll have to bottle-feed them until their mum gets better and she remembered how soppy you are about baby animals so..."

"Whoopeee!" I yelled, jumping up from the table and sending my fork flying. "Too right I'll help out!" This great big enormous beam stretched over my face from ear to ear and I started jigging up and down in excitement. "Feeding baby lambs! Awesome!"

Stuart grinned at me. "Oh, that's a shame, I told her you would probably be too busy," he said. "I know you aren't really that keen on baby animals…"

"WHAT?!" I yelled, stopping dead still. "Are you mad?"

"He's winding you up," Dad said, patting me on the arm reassuringly. "Don't take any notice of him."

"Oh! Phew! Oh!" I said, smiling again. "Stu – you pig!"

"Talking of pigs, do you think you can finish your tea without flinging any more cutlery around?" Mum sighed. "I bet those farm animals have better table manners than you, Lyndsey Collins. Come on – the sooner you finish it off, the sooner you can phone Mrs Mack and talk about tomorrow."

Well, you've never seen anyone polish off three sausages, a pile of mash and a plate full of baked beans so quick before. No more talking – I just gobbled the lot down as if my life depended on it. But then I had to wait for everyone else to finish, and THEN I had to sit through pudding as well.

I was too excited to eat anything else but Mum wouldn't let me leave the table until everyone had finished eating. Manners again, you see! And that meant waiting for my little brother Ben, aged four, who's just the slowest eater in Cuddington. First, he made a well in his mashed potato. Then he scooped up all his beans and put them in the well. Then he said he didn't want any more and so I had to watch while Dad did the old "Open wide, here comes the choo-choo train" game to feed him mouthfuls of sausage. TYPICAL!

At long last, Mum said we could all leave the table, and us Sleepover girls went in the living room. "Yay!" I shouted, dancing around. "Isn't that cool about me going to bottle-feed those cute little lambs? Can you imagine?"

"Yeah, lucky thing," Rosie said. "I bet they're really cuddly and sweet."

"That's if they don't have fleas, of course," Fliss said, with a shudder. Like I told you, she's not big on nature.

"D'you know, I've never seen a real lamb before," Kenny said. "Well, apart from one with mint sauce and gravy on it, of course."

"Oh, KENNY!" everyone groaned.

"I've never even been on a FARM before," Frankie said, quickly changing the subject. "What's Mr Mackintosh's farm like?"

"Well, he's got loads of cows and sheep," I said, trying to remember. Then I had a brilliant idea. PING! Flashing lightbulb over the head! "Hey – why don't you lot come with me? Why don't we make it a Sleepover Club day at the farm?"

"Yeah!" "Coo-ell!" "Wicked!" Frankie, Rosie and Kenny shouted at once. But one person was silent.

"Fliss?" I said, turning to her. "Do you fancy it?"

"Well..." she began.

"I'm sure the lambs don't have fleas," Rosie said reassuringly. "Well, not too many anyway."

"And we won't let any cows try and eat you," Kenny said. "JOKE, Fliss!" she added quickly, as Fliss's mouth fell open in alarm.

"Go on, Fliss," I urged her. "We can see the ducklings. Stuart said there are loads. And there might be some cute little chicks!"

"Well..." she said again.

"And if you DON'T come, we'll tell everyone at school that you're scared of a few titchy-witchy baby lambs," Frankie said, raising her eyebrows threateningly.

"All right, all right," Fliss said at once. "And don't be so silly – of course I'm not scared of lambs."

"What about big angry bulls?" Kenny said, making little horns on her head with her fingers. "Big angry bulls that come CHARGING towards you!"

Fliss squealed and darted to the side as Kenny lowered her head and ran straight at her. "Kenny!" she squeaked. "What are you doing?"

Kenny lowered her head again and chased Fliss around the table. "Getting you ready for our day at the farm," she said, with a mischievous glint in her eye. "You can't let a bull see that you're scared of it, Fliss. They're like dogs – they can SMELL the fear, you know. MOOOOO!"

"Don't take any notice of her, Fliss," I said, pushing Kenny out of the way. "The bull won't hurt you."

"Just don't wear red," Frankie said warningly. "They hate red."

"What about navy blue?" Fliss asked at once, looking worried. "Do they hate navy blue? Because I was going to wear my blue jacket tomorrow and..."

"Navy blue, did you say?" Rosie said. She shook her head anxiously. "Ooh, no. Bulls HATE navy blue. It sends them crazy."

"No, it doesn't, Fliss, she's teasing," I said, as Fliss was starting to look terrified. The last thing I wanted was for her to back out of the whole thing. "Honestly, trust me, we don't even have to go NEAR the bull. We don't even have to look at it! Now, don't anyone say anything else horrible to Fliss while I phone Mrs Mack. I mean it! And anyway, she might not say you lot can come at all."

They all went quiet at that. Ha! The power of Lyndz! I didn't mean to be bossy but I knew that if Fliss got too flustered and scared, she'd put her foot down and wouldn't come with us. And Fliss gets very stubborn when she wants to. I quickly dialled the farm number before anyone said anything in return.

"Mrs Mackintosh, hello, it's Lyndsey Collins here," I said when she answered. "Stuart told me about the lambs – how are they?"

"Not so bad, just missing their mummy," she replied. "They were born a bit early so they're quite small, and they need lots of looking after, which is why I was wondering if you'd like to help me feed them. What do you think? Could you spare a bit of time tomorrow to come over?"

"Yes, PLEASE!" I said at once. Mrs Mack was asking me like she thought I'd be doing her a favour, when really it was going to be the best treat I'd had in ages. "But the only thing is, I'm having a sleepover with some friends tonight. Would they... er... would you mind... could they...?" I didn't quite know how to ask without sounding dead cheeky.

"Oh, bring them along with you if they want to come," Mrs Mack said at once. "The more the merrier!"

I grinned at the others and made the thumbs-up sign. "Are you sure? Oh, that's brilliant. Thank you!"

"Look forward to seeing you all tomorrow then," she said cheerily. "But bring some wellies, won't you? The farm's quite muddy at the moment."

"Will do," I said. I could hardly get the words out, I was feeling so excited. "See you tomorrow."

I put the phone down and twirled about happily. "Hooray!" I cheered.

"Let me guess, she said no, you can't bring your smelly sleepover friends along," Kenny joked.

"No, I bet she said you could bring all your NICE sleepover friends along, apart from that smelly Kenny McKenzie girl," Frankie said, sticking her tongue out at Kenny. "She didn't want the animals to be too, like, frightened."

"Nope, you're both wrong," I said. "We are sooo invited! We're all going to the farm. And we're going tomorrow. How about that?"

CHAPTER TWO

Coo-ell! Everyone started getting really excited about going to the farm, even Fliss. What a miracle! "I'm going to send my mum a text message to tell her," she announced importantly. Fliss got this wicked mobile in the summer, and uses it at every single opportunity. Her biggest complaint at the moment is that none of the rest of us have got mobiles yet, so she can't message any of us – but as she sees us nearly every day, I don't really know why she wants to.

"GOING 2 C LAMS TOM" she typed in laboriously, sticking her tongue out in concentration. If you hadn't guessed, Fliss isn't the best speller in the world. "Get it? Going to see lambs tomorrow. Clever, eh? There!" she said, pressing the Send button.

"Fliss, in the time it's taken you to send that, you could have actually phoned her and told her," Frankie pointed out. "In fact, you could have phoned six different people and told them."

"And 'lambs' has a 'b' at the end of it anyway," I told her.

Fliss looked scornful. "No, it doesn't!" she said. "Lambs? Where's the 'b' in that? I can't hear any 'b'!"

"That's 'cos it's silent, you big nana," said Rosie.

"The 'b' comes at the end, stoopid," Kenny said, writing it down. "Look!"

Fliss took one look and tossed the piece of paper aside. "You lot are always trying to wind me up," she declared, putting her nose in the air. "Well, not this time! Lam-b. As if! Lamb rhymes with ham, doesn't it? And I know how to spell ham. H, A, M. Right?"

I was just about to get the dictionary out

to prove it to her when Fliss's phone beeped. Her mum had messaged her back already.

"WHO IS TOM?" the message said. "AND DON'T EAT CLAMS – U R ALLERGIC."

"What is she on about?" Fliss wondered aloud. "Tom? Who IS Tom?"

"Tom's my brother," I said, giggling. "You meant 'tomorrow' but she thought you were talking about my brother!"

"And you told her you were going to 'C LAMS TOM'," Rosie laughed. "And she thought you meant CLAMS."

"Oh, honestly," Fliss grumbled. "She doesn't know how to spell lambs either."

Just then, Mum came in the room. "Fliss, dear, your mum's on the phone," she said, looking a bit bemused. "She said something about you being allergic to shellfish and not to eat any clams. I tried to tell her that we don't have any clams in the house but she insisted on speaking to you."

Fliss went off to reassure her mum that no, she wasn't going to eat any shellfish, she was just going to see some lambs – with a 'b' – and the rest of us all cracked up.

"Ahh, the wonders of text messaging," Frankie sniggered. "So quick and soooo confusing!"

Once Fliss was back, having cleared up the clams confusion, we decided to play some animal games to get us in a farm-visiting kind of mood for Saturday. First, we had a few rounds of Squeak, Piggy, Squeak. Have you ever played that? One person is blindfolded and they blunder about the room until they bump into someone else. The blindfolded person then says, "Squeak, Piggy, Squeak!" When the person they've caught does squeak, they have to guess who it is. It's really funny, especially all the pig impressions.

It was even funnier than usual this night when my dad walked into the room in the middle of a game. He saw what we were up to and knelt down so that he was the same height as us. Then when blindfolded Frankie bumped into him and told him, "Squeak, Piggy, squeak", he went, "SQUEAK! SQUEAK!" in such a loud, un-squeaky voice, Frankie nearly fell over in surprise. We all burst out laughing and Frankie pulled off her blindfold to see who'd made such a noise. When she saw that it was my dad, she laughed too. "Naughty piggy!" she giggled, wagging a finger at him. "Big daddy piggy made Frankie piggy jump!"

Next we played Farmer In The Den, which got so loud, my mum came in my bedroom to see what all the noise was about. "I thought you'd invited twenty real farmers round," she said. "Is there really only you five in here making all that din?"

"Sorry, Mum," I said, but she was twinkling at me, so I knew she didn't really mind.

Then we decided to play Piggy In The Middle which turned out to be even noisier. Instead of there being one piggy in the middle of two people, the poor person who was the piggy in this game had to work twice as hard to try and catch the teddy bear the other four of us were throwing to each other. Super-fit Kenny was the first piggy and even she was struggling to catch hold of it. She went running back and forth as the teddy was tossed, jumped up high to try and catch it, and even dived to the floor a couple of times.

"Come on, lazy piggy, you can do it," Fliss taunted her, waving the teddy above her head.

Kenny charged towards her, but just at the last minute – whoosh! Fliss threw the teddy over her head to Rosie, who caught it neatly.

"Oh, pigg-eeee, where are you?" Rosie sang. "Come and get the tedd-eee!"

Whoosh! Away went the teddy again, this time to me.

"Too slow!" Rosie crowed.

Kenny was starting to get frustrated. And nobody, but nobody calls her "too slow" if they want to live to see next Christmas!

"You are soooo dead, Cartwright," she warned Rosie with one of her evil grins. Then she waited until Rosie had the teddy again, and steamed across, rugby-tackled her and wrestled her to the floor to try and get it.

"You cheat!" Frankie screamed and promptly dived in to help Rosie.

"Now who's too slow?" Kenny yelled, brandishing the teddy above her head. "Ha! Gotcha!"

We ended up getting so wild that going to sleep later that night was really difficult.

Frankie and Rosie kept putting on silly voices and asking Fliss to pass them the clams, and then we'd all giggle helplessly. Then once we'd all recovered and were lying quietly in the dark, someone else would explode with giggles – and we'd all be off again. Plus, I was far too excited about going to the farm to even THINK about sleeping.

Somehow, I managed it though. Just as I was thinking, there was no way I could possibly get to sleep, the next thing I knew it was morning and the sun was shining again. Hooray!

After breakfast, I told Mum what Mrs Mack had said about the farm being muddy and between us, we hunted out five pairs of wellies. I had my new blue ones, Rosie squashed her little tootsies into my old pair that were too small for me now, Kenny Big-Foot borrowed a pair of Tom's and Frankie wore a pair of my mum's. There was also an old pair of Stuart's boots that we offered Fliss, but she wasn't having any of it.

"No, thanks, I'm going to wear my new trainers," she said, waving a foot proudly to show us. "Nice, aren't they?"

"They are nice, Fliss, but they won't be for much longer if you wear them on the farm," my mum told her. "Honestly, love, you'll get them covered in mud."

"Well, I won't go in any mud," Fliss said promptly. "Thanks, Mrs Collins, and I don't want to be rude but I really don't want to wear those wellies."

"It's up to you," my mum said, putting them back in the cupboard. "But I don't want your mum phoning me up tonight, all upset because your new trainers are ruined."

"Oh, she won't," Fliss said confidently. "Because there is no way I'm going to set foot in any yucky mud, and that's that!"

CHAPTER THREE

Confident words from Fliss, all right, but as soon as Dad dropped us off at the farm, she realised she was going to have to EAT those words. Mrs Mackintosh hadn't been exaggerating about the mud – it was everywhere, even all the way up from the garages to the farmhouse door!

Squelch! Squelch! Squelch! Me, Rosie, Kenny and Frankie happily splodged through the mud up to the house. We turned round to see Fliss slithering about behind us, trying to stay on her tiptoes as thick brown mud splurged around her gleaming white trainers.

Mrs Mack pulled open the front door. "Hello, Lyndsey, hello, girls," she said with a warm smile. Mrs Mack is ALWAYS smiling. She's one of the jolliest people I've ever met. Mind you, she looked almost serious for a moment when she caught sight of Fliss, still halfway up to the door, trying desperately to tread on the grassy bits. "Oh dear," she said thoughtfully. "I think I'm going to have to find a spare pair of welly boots for someone, aren't I?"

"Look at her," Kenny giggled. "Hey, Poo-Foot! Get a move on!"

Fliss glared at her. "This is sooo gross," she moaned. "I feel sick!"

Once Fliss had made it into the farmhouse and Mrs Mack had persuaded her to swap her trainers – which already looked as if Fliss had been stuck in a bog – for a pair of boots, she took us all into the big, warm farm kitchen. "Now come and see the two new members of the Mackintosh family, a boy and a girl," she said, bringing us over to a cardboard box. "Oh, they're having a sleep right now. Can you see?"

The five of us knelt on the stone floor to peer into the box. And there, fast asleep and all curled up, were two darling little lambs. They were both pure, pure white apart from their black noses, and they looked all small and helpless. Without thinking, my hand just went straight in and stroked one of them very gently. Soooo cuddly and soft!

"Oh!" I said. "He's so... woolly!"

"Derr... really?" Kenny said sarcastically, but even she was reaching a hand in to stroke a soft little coat. "Ahhh... look at this one's tiny little ears."

"What are they called?" Rosie asked Mrs Mack.

"Well, do you know, I haven't given them names yet," she replied. "Maybe you girls would like to think of something to call them?"

"Snowy," said Frankie at once.

Fliss pulled a face. "That's sooo boring," she said. "Our neighbour's cat is called Snowy."

"We used to have a rabbit called Snowy, too," I added.

"How about... Poo-Foot?" Kenny giggled. "Oh, no – we already know someone called that, don't we, Fliss?"

"Stop calling me that, Kenny," Fliss said crossly. "No one thinks it's funny."

Fliss was starting to look a bit upset. You can always tell because her bottom lip starts turning down, and her cheeks get a bit pink.

"Hmmm... what about Snowdrop, then?" Rosie suggested quickly, looking at a pot of snowdrops that Mrs Mack had on one of the windowsills.

"Snowdrop is a cute name," I agreed, twitching one of the lambs' ears. "You can be Snowdrop, little one! What do you think, Fliss?"

Fliss shrugged, still in a narky mood. "Whatever," she sniffed.

"What about this one, then?" Frankie said, stroking Snowdrop's little sister. "Look, she's got a tiny bit of black on her face. How about... er..."

"Snowflake," I said.

"Cornflake," Kenny joked. "Or chocolate

Flake! Hey, Flake-brain, what do you think of your new name?"

"Don't be so stoooopid, Kenny," Fliss said, rolling her eyes.

"How about naming her after another flower to go with Snowdrop?" Frankie suggested. "How about Crocus?"

"Sounds like a frog's name!" I said. "Croak-us – get it?"

"How about Jasmine?" Rosie said.

"That's pretty," Fliss said. "Snowdrop and Jasmine – don't they sound sweet?"

Ooh! Just as she said that, the two tiny lambs started waking up. "Oh, look, they know their names already," I said in delight. "Hello, Snowdrop. Hello, Jasmine!"

Snowdrop stood up on his wobbly little legs and pushed his nose into Mrs Mack's hand. Then he bleated plaintively. Ma-a-a-a! he went.

"Someone's hungry, by the sound of it," Mrs Mack said, giving him a friendly stroke. "I'll just warm up your bottle, Snowdrop."

Then Jasmine started bleating too. Maaaa-aaa-aa! Maa-aa-aa! I couldn't resist any more and picked her up to cuddle her. "Oh, hungry baby, it won't be long," I crooned into her little ear. Honestly, my heart was just MELTING as I held her warm little body. Then she snuggled her head into my neck and I thought I would burst with happiness!

"Jasmine, that tickles," I giggled. "Ooh, don't try and nibble my ear – that isn't your food, you know!"

Luckily, Mrs Mack brought over two warm bottles of milk at that moment so my ear was saved just in time. "Here we are," she said. "One for Jasmine, Lyndsey. And who wants to feed Snowdrop?"

"Me!"

"Oh, I do!"

"Yes, please!"

"Can I?"

The other four all spoke at once. "Eeny, meeny, miny, moe – Frankie gets it," Mrs Mack said, passing her the bottle. "Don't worry – you'll all get a turn before long. They are both very hungry lambs!"

Seconds later, I was cuddled up with Jasmine, and Frankie was feeding Snowdrop.

The lambs sucked away contentedly and we felt like a pair of proud old mums! "Good girl," I said, patting Jasmine's head gently as she guzzled down the milk. "You WERE hungry, weren't you?"

"Well done, girls," Mrs Mack told us as the lambs slurped up the last of the milk. "That'll keep their tummies nice and full for a bit. Now – who wants to help me collect the eggs?"

"Yay!" we all said at once, grinning at each other.

"Come on, I'll give you a little tour of the farm," Mrs Mack said as we put our wellies on again and went outside. "Chickens first – let's see if there are any eggs for Mr Mackintosh's breakfast tomorrow morning."

As we went out the back door, Fliss nearly trod on a chicken that was pecking at the ground in front of her. "Chook! Chook! Chook!" it said, rushing away at once.

"Oh yes, I forgot to warn you about that one," Mrs Mack said, smiling at Fliss's startled face. "She always gets under my feet too, the silly thing! I let the chickens wander around wherever they want, you see, and that one is always trying to sneak in the house."

"Do you ever let them in?" I asked, imagining what it would be like to have dinner with a chicken clucking around your toes. Or how about trying to watch telly with a chicken sitting next to you on the sofa?!

"Do I heck!" Mrs Mack snorted. "I'd be finding the daft things all over the place if I left the back door open for five minutes. I made that mistake once last summer – and half an hour later, there was one chicken in the downstairs loo, and one in my pantry." She laughed at the memory.

I couldn't help thinking how much fun it would be to find a chicken in your bathroom. I decided straight away that when I was older and had my own farm, I was going to let ALL the animals wander in and out of my house. Cats, dogs, lambs, chickens, pigs... all would be welcome to snuggle up with me in my home.

I was pleased to see that the chickens lived in a cute little hut with lots of comfy straw spread around for nesting. Ever since I saw the film *Chicken Run*, I've been worried that chickens don't have very nice lives, especially ones that are all squashed up in little coops. But the ones on the Mackintosh farm seemed to be happy wandering around in the sunshine, pecking busily away at grain.

As we went up to the hut, we could hear a great squawking coming from inside. "Sounds to me like someone's just laid an egg," Mrs Mack told us. "Can you hear? Chickens always make a lot of noise when they lay one because they want to let the cockerel know how clever they are."

"Oh, there he is – Rocky the rooster!" Frankie said, pointing to the cockerel who had a bright red wobbly comb on his head. He was strutting around, looking all important. As soon as he saw us, he let out a bloodcurdling "Cock-a-doodle-dooooo!"

Fliss nearly jumped out of her skin. "I don't think he likes us," she said, trying to hide behind Rosie. "He's a bit fierce, isn't he?"

"Oh, he's all hot air," Mrs Mack said, shooing him away from us. "He wouldn't hurt a fly, really. Now, let's go in and see if that racket really was an egg being laid."

Inside the chicken hut, there was one fat chicken who scuttled off as soon as we all trooped in. "Ah yes, just as I thought," said Mrs Mack, picking up an egg from one of the boxes of hay. "A nice brown egg, still warm. Who wants to hold it?"

"Me, please," Kenny said at once, holding her hand out. She passed it around so we could all feel how warm it was.

"Be careful, won't you, because eggs that have just been laid still have a soft shell," said Mrs Mack. "Give it a gentle prod – gently, I said, Frankie! See what I mean? The shell is still quite flexible, isn't it?"

"Weird!" Frankie agreed. "It's all... rubbery."

"Oh, look – there's another one," Rosie said, pointing to a box a bit further down.

"And there's another!" I said, catching sight of an egg that was half-hidden by straw. This was as good as a treasure hunt.

Altogether, we found ten eggs and Mrs Mack was pleased. "Some of the chickens have got into the bad habit of laying eggs all over the farm," she told us. "You sometimes find them in the strangest places. One night, I left my peg bag lying around after I'd put the washing out to dry. Next morning, there was a lovely brown egg inside it, nestled among the pegs!"

After the chicken hut, we went over to the cow sheds.

"Ooh, Mrs Mackintosh, can we see the cows being milked?" Kenny asked at once, bouncing up and down. "I've always wanted to see that."

"Sorry, girls, you're too late," Mrs Mackintosh told us. "The cows are all back in the fields again now. We bring them in first thing to be milked, and then again in the evening. And much as I'd love to have you here all day, I expect your mums might want you home again."

"Ohhh!" we all groaned.

"They won't mind," I said quickly. Suddenly, I really REALLY wanted to see the cows being milked too. I'd never really thought about it before. I'd just poured the

39

milk on to my cereal every morning, or poured out a glass of it to drink. But seeing milk actually come out of a cow... that would have been awesome!

"Sorry, girls," she said, seeing our disappointed faces. "But your dad's coming to pick you up again after lunch, isn't he, Lyndsey?"

"Oh yeah," I said. "I've got a riding lesson this afternoon. I'd completely forgotten about it." That shows you what a good time I was having on the farm. Horse riding is usually my number one favourite thing to do, and the fact that somehow I'd managed to FORGET about it...

"There you go, then. That'll be much more fun than seeing our cows," Mrs Mack said, as we went through to the sheds. "Now, this is what we call the milking parlour. The cows go through one at a time, and these machines milk them for us. All the milk gets collected in here" – she pointed to a huge tank – "and then we take it along to the dairy down the road."

"Awesome!" Kenny said, squatting down to get a better look. "Wow – I bet these machines are well noisy when they're going full pelt, aren't they?"

Before Mrs Mackintosh could reply, a voice came from behind us. "Hello – here comes trouble." We all looked round to see Mr Mackintosh and Stuart.

"How are they getting on?" asked Stuart. "I hope they're behaving themselves."

"Cheek!" said Frankie. "The Sleepover Club always behaves beautifully. Ask anyone."

Stuart laughed in disbelief. "Yeah, right, Frankie," he said. "In your dreams!"

"Actually, it's a pleasure to have them," Mrs Mackintosh told him. "It's lovely to have some girls around the place. Makes a nice change." She leaned over to us. "You know, I always wanted a daughter of my own. And what did I end up with? Three sons!"

"That's bad luck," Kenny said, shaking her head. "Every house needs a few girls around. Especially girls as cool as the Sleepover Club!"

Mrs Mack frowned at that. "What is this Sleepover Club, anyway?" she asked. "I've heard you mention it a few times now."

Frankie explained it to her.

"So you've had sleepovers in all sorts of places then, have you?" Mrs Mack asked at the end.

"Oh yeah – in a museum, in a blitz house, in a Scottish castle... you name it, we've been there," Kenny said proudly.

"How about a farm?" Mrs Mack asked, smiling broadly at us. "Have you ever had a sleepover on a farm before?"

We shook our heads. Did she mean...? Was she about to...?

"Well, why didn't you say so before?" she cried. "How about I invite you to a sleepover on the Mackintosh farm – and then you can get up early with us to help milk the cows?"

CHAPTER FOUR

"Can we sleep in hay, like the chickens do?" Kenny shouted excitedly.

Mrs Mack laughed at her eager face. "Certainly not!" she said. "It's only March – you'd freeze to death. No – you can sleep in the attic room where the boys used to sleep. That'll be much cosier, and you can make as much noise as you want up there."

Fliss looked thankful at that. "Why would anyone want to sleep in hay?" she asked, pulling a face. "All those beetles and spiders! Kenny – you're seriously weird, you know."

"Seriously weird is better than being seriously WET, Poo-Foot," Kenny retorted. "It would have been a right laugh, having hay fights all night!"

Fliss looked as if she'd just been slapped. "Stop calling me that," she said in a shaky voice. "It's not funny." Now she really DID look as if she was going to cry. Then she pulled out her mobile and started typing in a text message.

"Who are you messaging?" I asked, feeling sorry for her. Sometimes Kenny goes a bit far. She never knows when to stop – and then, before you know it, it's too late and Fliss is blubbing her eyes out.

"My mum," Fliss said, her lip wobbling a bit. "I'm asking her to come and take me home. I'd forgotten that we're meant to be er... going out this afternoon."

She didn't look me in the eye and I didn't believe her for a second. Poor old Fliss had obviously had enough teasing for one day. I looked over at Kenny, who had folded her arms across her chest and was looking scornful.

"Let's go and see the duck pond before you have to go home then," Mrs Mack said, breaking up the awkward silence. "This way!"

I linked arms with Fliss as we went out of the main yard to the duck pond. I wasn't taking sides or anything, I just wanted to cheer her up a bit. Fliss doesn't cry half as much as she used to, but I could tell that one more mean remark from Kenny would set her off big time, and the flood-gates would open!

As soon as we got to the pond, one of the ducks swam to the side and waddled straight up to Mrs Mack, quacking noisily.

"This duck thinks he's a dog," Mrs Mack explained with a laugh, patting him gently on the head. "Sometimes he'll follow me around the farm all day, won't you?"

"QUACK!" said the duck proudly, as if he knew he was being talked about.

Fliss edged away. "He's looking at me funny," she said nervously. "Will he bite me?"

The rest of us roared with laughter at her. "Ducks don't have teeth, you silly moo," Frankie said, going up to pat the friendly dog-duck.

45

"Watch out for that beak, though," Kenny teased. "He might start nipping round your ankles like a real dog!"

"WOOF!" Rosie said and Fliss jumped, which made us all laugh again. Even the duck looked like he thought it was funny.

"Come on, you dozy duck, let's go back to see how those little lambs are," Mrs Mack said to him. And as we started walking away from the pond, back to the house, the duck came waddling along behind us. It really did remind me of taking my dog, Buster, for a walk.

"Do you think he'll fetch a stick if I throw one?" Rosie joked. "Here, boy! Walkies!"

There was thick, gloopy mud the other side of the pond. Soon we were all clutching on to each other, trying not to fall over in it.

"Good job you haven't still got your trainers on now, Fliss," Kenny said. "Or else you really would be a total P—"

"Don't you dare say that again or I'll push you in the mud!" Fliss snapped.

The rest of us blinked in surprise. I'd never heard Fliss sounding so fierce. "Just ignore her, Fliss, she's only messing around," I said, trying to make the peace.

Fliss's phone beeped then and she looked at it. "Oh good, it's Mum, she's on her way to get me," she said, tossing her long hair over her shoulders.

"Yeah, that is good," Kenny sniped back. "Good riddance if you can't take a joke!"

"Get lost, Kenny," Fliss snapped back.

"Oh, stop it, you two!" I said. I was starting to feel reeeeally embarrassed. This was awful!

"Yeah, stop it, Mrs Mack doesn't want to hear you two moaning minnies bickering away," Frankie ordered them.

Mrs Mack laughed as we took our boots off and went back into the kitchen. "Oh, don't you worry about me, I've heard it all before," she said. "I've got three sisters and I could tell you some right old stories about the fights we used to have. Hair-pulling, name-calling... oh, we were the most horrible girls you could imagine."

"Really?" said Kenny, sounding interested. "Coo-ell!"

I shuffled my feet, feeling awkward. "So does that mean... can we still have a sleepover on your farm?" I asked in a little voice. I was terrified Mrs Mack was going to change her mind now she'd seen how horrible WE could be.

"Of course!" she said warmly, putting her arm round me. "I'm looking forward to it already. How about next weekend?"

"Oh, yes PLEASE!" Kenny, Frankie, Rosie and I all said at once.

Fliss looked at the floor. "I think I'm busy that weekend," she mumbled, just as a car beeped its horn outside. "That's my mum, I'd better go. Thank you for having me, Mrs Mackintosh, I've had a lovely time. Bye, Lyndz. Bye, Rosie. Bye, Frankie."

As Mrs Mack went to show her out, the rest of us looked at each other. Too busy for a sleepover? Who was she trying to kid? No one, but *no one* missed a sleepover. Not unless they were about to die of a horrible disease or were going to be out of the country.

"She didn't even say bye to me," Kenny said, sounding a bit surprised.

"Well, you were pretty mean to her," I pointed out. Sometimes Kenny is a bit... how shall I put it?... thick-skinned.

"I was only TEASING!" Kenny said, rolling her eyes impatiently.

"WE know that, but Fliss can be a bit sensitive sometimes, can't she?" Rosie reminded her. Then she giggled. "Especially when you keep calling her Poo-Foot!"

"Poor, poor Poo-Foot," Frankie sniggered. "She'll cheer up once her mum's taken her out shopping this afternoon."

I bit my lip. I wasn't so sure. I hadn't seen Fliss blow up like that for absolutely ages.

We had one more cuddle with the lambs and gave them another bottle. Then my dad turned up to take us home. "Bye, Snowdrop, bye, Jasmine, be good, won't you?" I called. "Bye, Mrs Mack, see you next week."

Next week! Seeing the cows being milked! I couldn't wait. I even got told off in my riding lesson that afternoon for not being able to concentrate. Do you ever get that feeling where you're so happy, you feel like there

49

are little bubbles popping inside you? I was feeling so bubbly and cheerful that even Kenny and Fliss's argument didn't seem like a big deal any more. They'll get over it fast enough, I told myself. By Monday morning at school, it'll all be forgotten. But I was wrong. Boy, was I ever wrong!

It wasn't until Monday morning that I realised that the argument truly WASN'T all forgotten. Usually us five are on the phone to each other all the time at the weekend. Sure enough, I spoke to Frankie, Rosie and Kenny at different times on Saturday night and Sunday. Not Fliss though. I meant to give her a ring, but what with horse riding, helping Mum make the Sunday dinner, playing with my baby brother and taking Buster for a long walk in the park, I just ran out of time. Never mind, I thought, we'll catch up at school instead.

But when I got to school on Monday, the first thing I saw was Fliss chatting away with Alana Banana and Katie Parker, two other girls from our class. Strange, I thought.

Normally us five all get together in the playground and have a good gossip before we go into school.

"Hiya, Fliss!" I said, tapping her on the shoulder. "All right?"

"Oh, hi, Lyndz," she said coolly. Then she turned her back on me and carried on talking to Alana.

I stood there open-mouthed. Fliss had just turned her back on me! I couldn't believe it. "Fliss?" I asked, feeling confused. "Are you OK?"

"Yes, fine, thanks," she said, in that same cool voice. And once again, she turned away from me, ignoring me.

Luckily, just at that moment, I spotted Frankie and Kenny walking into the playground. "Oh, there are the others," I said, feeling relieved. "Coming?"

"No, thank you," she said over her shoulder. This time she didn't even look at me. "Bye."

I stood there like I was frozen to the spot. In the end, Alana turned round to me. "Look, dumbo, don't you get the message?

She don't wanna know you. All right?" she said.

"Right," I answered, not sure what else to say. "Well... er... bye, then."

Fliss ignored me again. Then, as I walked off, the three of them started giggling and whispering together.

I felt sick. What was happening? Didn't Fliss want to be friends any more? Now it was my turn to want to burst into tears. The way she'd looked at me had been awful. Like she hated me. Like I was the most horrid little worm in the world.

Then a truly terrible thought popped into my head. *What if Fliss didn't want to be in the Sleepover Club any more?*

CHAPTER FIVE

That Monday really did feel like one of the most horrible days of my life. Normally, us five sit on a table together in school – but not on this day. As soon as we were all in the classroom, Fliss asked Mrs Weaver if she could swap places and sit with Alana and Katie instead of us. Mrs Weaver raised her eyebrows in surprise but didn't ask why, just said yes. Of course, our biggest enemies the M&Ms stuck their noses in straight away.

"Ooh, had a little tiff, have we, girls?" Emma Hughes said, smirking in glee.

"Ahh, diddums, the Tripover Club aren't *fwends* any more," Emily Berryman sneered.

"Yes, we are," I said at once.

"No, we are NOT!" Fliss retorted haughtily.

I stared at her in disbelief, but she didn't look back at me.

"Ooh, DEAR!" the M&Ms sniggered. "Someone's got their knick-knicks in a twist!"

"I'll put your necks in a twist if you don't shut your traps right now," Kenny growled at them.

"That's quite enough of that, ladies, thank you very much," Mrs Weaver said firmly. "I don't want World War Three breaking out in my classroom, if it's all the same to you. Now then – did everyone have a nice weekend? Who would like to tell the class what they did?"

Nearly everyone put their hands up, as usual. I couldn't help noticing that Fliss was one of the few people who didn't. She just sat there, picking at her nail varnish as if she'd had the most boring weekend possible.

"Yes, Jack?"

"Miss, me and my dad went to see Man United," Jack said proudly. "It was wicked, we won four-nil and afterwards, we went and had a burger and chips."

"Sounds very exciting. David? What did you get up to?"

"It was my brother's birthday and we went swimming with his friends," David said. "And I pushed my sister in and we had a big water fight. And then we had birthday cake and ice cream and chips!"

"That sounds a delicious mixture," Mrs Weaver laughed. "Kenny, how about you? Anything nice?"

"We had a sleepover at Lyndsey's and then went to a farm," Kenny said, grinning at the memory. "We fed some baby lambs and saw some ducks and collected eggs from the chickens."

"How lovely!" said Mrs Weaver. "Emma, what did you do this weekend?"

I looked over at Fliss while Emma rattled on about going to ballet or something. Fliss hadn't even looked up while Kenny had talked about going to the farm, just carried on picking at her nail varnish and looking bored. I desperately wanted to catch her eye, to smile at her, or even to ask if she was OK. But she wouldn't look anywhere near us. What was going on? Was this all because of her stupid argument with Kenny?

The morning dragged on while everyone in the class told their news. Finally, it got round to Fliss.

"Felicity, what did you do?" Mrs Weaver asked.

Fliss tossed her hair back. "I went shopping with my mum, Miss," was all she said.

"Anything else?"

"She bought me a new pair of shoes, Miss," Fliss added.

That was it. Didn't mention the sleepover, didn't mention going to the farm, nothing. I felt really, really sad. Fliss had been in a mood with Kenny before but never like this. It had never been so bad that she wouldn't talk to the rest of us, wouldn't sit with us, wouldn't even look at us. Kenny would have to make friends with her fast, she just HAD to. I wouldn't be able to bear much more of this awful silent treatment.

As soon as it was playtime, me and Rosie went over and tried to talk to Fliss, but she wasn't having any of it.

"Please!" I begged her. "Don't be like this, Fliss! Kenny's really sorry, honest she is."

Fliss looked over at Kenny, who was chasing two boys round the playground and shouting rude names at them at the top of her voice. "Yeah, she really looks sorry," she said sarcastically.

"Well, you don't have to be mad at us as well," Rosie argued. "We haven't done anything wrong, we're still your friends."

"Mmm," Fliss said. "But you're always ganging up with Kenny when she picks on me. You all like Kenny more than you like me!"

"No, we don't!" I said hotly. "Why do you think that?" I could feel tears pricking the back of my eyes. I hate arguments, they really upset me. Silly arguments with my brothers are bad enough, but an argument with Fliss, one of my best friends, someone

I've known since we were in the infants together... It was awful.

"I've just had enough of everyone being mean to me and teasing me," Fliss said, sticking her nose in the air. "I don't want to be in the Sleepover Club any more and that's that! All you do is laugh at me and say mean things about me. That's not what I call good friends."

"Oh, Fliss!" I gulped, looking at her in horror. "Don't say that!" But she looked away.

"Fliss, don't be like that," Rosie said. "We promise we won't be mean to you again. We tease you because we like you, that's all. If it upsets you, then we'll stop doing it. But you can't leave the Sleepover Club – it wouldn't be the same without you."

"No, it wouldn't," I agreed. "We'd all miss you, Fliss. We'd really really miss you."

"Kenny wouldn't," she said. She looked sad for just a split second, then her face went all tight and hard again. "Anyway, I've got some new friends now. Come on, Alana, come on, Katie, I'll tell you all about these new shoes my mum got me."

And off she went. Me and Rosie just stared after her in shock.

"I can't believe it," I said after a few moments. "She can't leave the Sleepover Club just like that. I won't let her!"

"I think it might be too late for that," Rosie said, shrugging her shoulders. "I think she already has."

"This is terrible," I moaned. "Quick, where are Frankie and Kenny? We need to make a plan, to get things back to normal again – quickly!"

Before we could speak to them though, the whistle blew and we had to go back into the classroom. It wasn't until lunchtime that Rosie and I could tell Frankie and Kenny what had happened. They couldn't believe the news either.

"I was only trying to have a bit of fun. She didn't have to take it all so seriously!" Kenny groaned. "What's she like? I think the M&Ms are right for once in their lives – Fliss really has got her knickers in a twist this time."

"That's not the point. The point is that she's dead upset and wants to leave the

Sleepover Club," Frankie said. "And we've got to make her realise how important she is to us. She's our mate! We don't want her going off with dopey Alana and vain-brain Katie."

"Exactly," I agreed. "So how do we make friends with her again?"

"Honestly, I only called her Poo-Foot a few times," Kenny was still grumbling. "She is sooo not fun sometimes. What's all the fuss about anyway? I think we should leave her to stew for a bit. She'll get over it."

"No, Kenny, she won't," Rosie argued. "We all know how stubborn Fliss is! She thinks we've all been ganging up on her and teasing her too much. She doesn't want to know us right now – I can't see her 'getting over it' just like that."

"We could write her a letter," Frankie said. "Saying sorry and all that."

"She might not even read it," I said. "She might just throw it in the bin."

"I think I should go and have it out with her," Kenny said, getting up. "I'll just tell her she's making a big fuss about nothing, and..."

"No!" I said in alarm.

"Don't you dare!" Frankie said at the same time.

"That would just make it a zillion times worse," Rosie agreed. "She is so not in the mood for another ruck with you."

Kenny sat down again, huffing and puffing. "Well, what then?" she said sarcastically. "Shall I get on my knees and beg her to please please per-leeeeze forgive me?"

"You might have to at this rate," Rosie said gloomily. "One thing's for sure – it's going to take more than a little 'sorry'."

"We could write her a poem," Frankie suggested. "She loves that kind of thing, doesn't she?"

"Yeah, good idea," I said. "And it'll show her we're really making an effort."

"Definitely," agreed Rosie. "Let's think. How shall we start off?"

Everyone started thinking. "Fliss, Fliss, don't be mad..." I began.

"If you leave us, we'll be sad," Frankie said.

We all sat in silence for a minute, trying to think of another line. "Little Poo-Foot, let's make friends..." Kenny started.

"No!" the rest of us shouted at once.

"How about, 'We want you to be our friend, and come to the farm with us next weekend'?" Rosie suggested.

"Brilliant!" I laughed. "Two more lines should do it. Let's think..."

"Sorry if we made you blue..." Frankie said.

"Let's make friends 'cos we love you," I added. "How about that?"

Kenny pulled a face. "Too soppy," she declared. "WAY too soppy."

"Fliss loves a bit of soppiness," I said firmly. "And anyway, do you want to sort this out or what?"

"Well, yes, but..." Kenny started.

"Well, we've got to be nice to her, then, haven't we?" I told her. "Anyone would think you want to stir it up even more!"

"Who, me?" Kenny grinned. "Stir up trouble? That is so not fair, Miss Collins!"

"I think a bit of soppiness might do the trick," Rosie said. "Let's write it out nicely for her and leave it in her tray."

So Frankie wrote the poem out in her best handwriting.

Fliss, Fliss, don't be mad
If you leave us, we'll be sad
We want you to be our friend
And come to the farm with us
next weekend
Sorry if we made you blue
Let's make friends 'cos we love you!

"That'll do the trick," Kenny said. "She's gonna love it, I bet you. You wait, we'll all be laughing about this tomorrow."

"Oh, I hope so," I said, crossing my fingers. "I really, really hope so!"

CHAPTER SIX

The plan was that we'd leave our 'sorry' poem in Fliss's tray so that she could find it and read it in her own time. But if you've ever read any other Sleepover books, you'll know that even our most brilliant plans often don't work out quite right. And this one certainly didn't.

I don't know how they knew what we were up to – they must have been spying on us, is my bet – but somehow those stinky M&Ms got wind of our plan. Later that afternoon, about an hour after Kenny had secretly put the poem into Fliss's tray, we could hardly believe our ears when we heard two sneering voices from the other side of the classroom.

"Fliss, Fliss, don't be mad," Emma started, and then threw back her head and laughed. "Too late for THAT anyway – if you ask me, she's been soft in the head for ages, old Flissy-wissy-pants."

I looked at the others. Oh no! How had Emma managed to get hold of our precious poem?

"Give that back," Frankie ordered. "It's not for you, it's for Fliss!"

"If you leave us, we'll be sad," Emily continued in a silly voice. "Oh boo-hoo-hoo, Sleepover Club – anyone ever tell you that you already ARE sad? What a bunch of losers!"

"We want you to be our friend," Emma read on. "Yeah – 'cos no one else will, will they? Hear that? They're so desperate for some mates now, they have to beg people, ha ha!"

I looked over at Fliss anxiously, only to see her glaring furiously at us. Her look said it all – she thought we were making fun of her again!

"Yes, do please please come to the farm next weekend," Emily said, reading from the page between guffaws. "Did I say farm? No – I meant zoo, where all the other weird animals are!"

"Excuse me, girls, what's going on?" Mrs Weaver said crossly. "I thought you were meant to be writing about your weekend, not giggling over a bit of paper. What is that, anyway?"

"It's a love poem, Miss," Emma said, turning bright red with giggles. "It's a stoopid, soppy love poem. Yuck!"

"Stop being so silly, Emma, and bring it here," Mrs Weaver ordered. "At once."

"Please, Miss, it's mine," I said desperately. I really didn't want Mrs Weaver to see it and embarrass us – not to mention Fliss – even more.

"Is it really, Lyndsey?" Mrs Weaver said icily. "Perhaps you could share it with the rest of the class, so we can all be entertained by it."

I went bright red and opened and shut my mouth like a goldfish. This was getting worse by the minute! "It's... it's private," I said in a small voice.

"Oh, really?" Mrs Weaver said. "Well, you should have thought about that before you started passing it round the class, shouldn't you?"

"But I didn't—" I started, but she wasn't listening.

"Be quiet, Lyndsey! Will somebody please bring me that piece of paper?" said Mrs Weaver in her scariest, don't-mess voice.

Emma was only too willing to go up with our special poem and wave it under Mrs Weaver's nose. Mrs Weaver read it quickly and then looked at me again. "And this was written by you, was it, Lyndsey?" she asked.

"Er, yes," I stammered. "Me and Rosie and Frankie and Kenny."

"Right," she said. "Well, perhaps you four can stay inside when it's playtime and you can explain why you thought it was a good idea to pass notes around when you should be getting on with your work."

"Yes, Miss," I said, lowering my eyes. I didn't dare look at Fliss again because I knew, sure as eggs are eggs, that she'd be absolutely boiling mad at us. I just knew she'd think we were playing some kind of mean trick to show her up in front of the whole class. And if there's one thing Fliss hates, it's being shown up – especially when Ryan Scott's in the room.

I told you this day got worse and worse, didn't I? When it came to playtime and everyone went outside except us four, I was expecting things to get worse still, with a roasting from Mrs Weaver. But to our surprise, she was actually quite nice. She asked us why we'd written the poem in the first place, and why we'd fallen out with Fliss.

Once we'd told her everything – and made sure we'd grassed up the M&Ms by making it clear that we'd left the poem in Fliss's tray, not passed it around the class – Mrs Weaver looked thoughtful. "It was very naughty of Emma and Emily to read your poem out loud," she said. "And it's a very nice poem, too – well done, girls. What a shame that all your hard work has been spoiled."

"Now Fliss is just going to think we were taking the mickey out of her," I sighed. "Which means she'll hate us even more."

"I'm sure I could explain it to her if you want me to," Mrs Weaver said. "Would you like me to try?"

We looked at each other. "Well, it couldn't make things any worse," Frankie reasoned.

"As long as you do it in private," Kenny said to Mrs Weaver. "Fliss hates any fuss, you know."

"I will be very private and very discreet," Mrs Weaver promised. "Leave it to me."

As we went outside for the rest of playtime, I couldn't help feeling worried, though. With Mrs Weaver involved now, Fliss might think we were trying to get her into trouble, or...

"Don't worry, Lyndz," Rosie said. "I'm sure it'll be all right."

"Yeah, Mrs Weaver is pretty cool," Kenny said. "I trust her not to muck this one up even more."

Even so, I couldn't help feeling nervous when I saw Mrs Weaver come outside and call Fliss over to her. I got that sick feeling back in my tummy when the two of them started talking. I know the way Fliss thinks, and I was willing to bet every penny in my piggy bank that she would be cursing the lot of us at that second.

As soon as Mrs Weaver had finished talking to her, we all nudged each other to see what would happen next. Would Fliss come over to us and make friends again? Say that now Mrs Weaver had explained the mix-up with the poem, everything was OK, and we were forgiven?

No. She went straight over to Alana and Katie, without even looking at us. Great. Another plan had backfired on us. So now what would we do?

Frankie was shaking her head. "Fliss can be so stubborn sometimes," she said. "We should have known it was going to take more than a poem to change her mind."

Kenny groaned. "I still say she's taking it all too seriously," she said. "Get over it, Fliss! So I called her a few stoopid names. Big deal! It's not like I just killed her grandma or anything, is it?"

"Well, we've tried speaking to her, we've tried a poem," I said. "How about..." And then my eyes lit up as I had an idea. Kerching! "What does Fliss love most in the world?" I said excitedly.

"Her clothes," Rosie said.

"Her shoes," Frankie said.

"Ryan Scott," Kenny said, pulling a face.

"No," I said, grinning. "Her mobile! Why don't we send her a text message? I bet she'll be so pleased to finally get a message from someone, that it'll cheer her up a ton – even when she sees it's from us!"

"Good idea, Lyndz," Rosie said approvingly. "She's been dying for us to text her. Perfect!"

"Well, it would be a good idea, if one of us had a mobile phone," Frankie pointed out. "Who do we know who's got one that we could borrow?"

"My sister, Tiff, has one," Rosie said at once. "She won't mind if I say it's an emergency. How about if we all go round to mine after school and bombard Fliss with messages saying how sorry we are? She won't be able to resist!"

"I tell you one thing, we'll definitely get a reply out of her too," I said. "She so loves that phone of hers that she'll jump at the chance to use it, even if it's just to reply to us lot."

"Sorted," Frankie said happily. "Operation Fliss is back on track!"

"Not for me, it isn't," Kenny said. "I've got swimming club after school tonight. We're doing the next lifesavers' badge so I can't miss it." Then she frowned. "Not that I get many chances to save any lives round here of course. I wish Cuddington was nearer the sea. Then I might be able to save more drowning people."

"Yeah, 'cos it would be absolutely lovely to see more people drowning, wouldn't it?" Rosie said sarcastically. "It would really brighten the place up – not. Kenny, you're awful!"

"I know," Kenny said with a grin. "But wouldn't life be boring without me?"

"Come on, evil Kenny," Frankie said, as the whistle blew. "Time to go back into school. Time to see if Fliss will speak to us again!"

Well, Mrs Weaver obviously hadn't done too great a job at talking Fliss round. She still wouldn't even look at us, let alone say anything. The rest of that day at school felt pretty miserable. I don't know if you've ever fallen out with one of your best friends so badly that they don't want to speak to you, but take it from me, it's not good news.

Finally, it was the end of school and we could go round to Rosie's to try out our text messaging plan. Kenny went off to the swimming baths on her bike but promised she'd drop in on her way back to see how we'd got on. So it was all down to me, Frankie and Rosie to do the business and make peace.

"I have an idea," Frankie said slowly as we walked to Rosie's house. "It's a bit of a naughty, sneaky idea but I reckon it might be our best move."

"Ooh, what?" Rosie and I said at once.

"Well, Fliss is mad with Kenny, right?" Frankie said. "And it's Kenny that she wants an apology from, really. So what do you say if Kenny sends a mega-grovelly text message to her?"

I shook my head. "No way," I said at once. "She won't do it. Kenny's as stubborn as Fliss, and if she thinks—"

"No," Frankie interrupted. "I don't mean that Kenny has to actually send the message herself. I mean that—"

"You mean we can send one for her!" Rosie jumped in, and then laughed out loud. "That's a brilliant idea! We send Fliss a message, supposedly from Kenny. Then Fliss will think that Kenny really IS sorry and will want to make friends again! Frank, you're a genius."

"I know," Frankie said modestly. "And this could be a lot of fun. I've always wanted to see Kenny grovelling, you know, and this is our chance." She grinned at the thought. "Let's make her really beg for forgiveness. Let's get her on those knees, begging like she's never begged before!"

CHAPTER
SEVEN

Sneaky or what? Frankie was right – it was a bit of a naughty plan and I hope you don't think we're all horrible girls for going along with it. But, like Frankie said, what Fliss really wanted was an apology from Kenny and this looked like being the only way on earth that she was going to get it!

We all felt dead giggly by the time we got back to Rosie's. That sort of nervous, excited giggliness where you're about to do something you know you really shouldn't. If Kenny had any idea of what we were up to, we'd totally be in the poo.

Rosie's big sister Tiffany was dead sweet about lending us her mobile, especially when we told her what we wanted it for. "Poor Fliss – yes, help yourself," she said. "Good luck."

"OK, what shall we say then?" Frankie said, with a mischievous glint in her eye. "Sorry, sorry, sorry, I'm on my knees, you're the greatest, love Kenny."

"How about 'I've been a complete moron'?" Rosie giggled. "We could really stitch Kenny up here!"

"She would absolutely kill us if she could hear us right now," I said, trying not to smirk at the thought of Kenny's furious face.

"I know, isn't it hilarious?" Frankie grinned. "Mind you, she wouldn't think twice about doing the same to one of us, would she? And trust me – she'll see the funny side. Even if she doesn't, Kenny never stays very mad with people for long."

In the end, after fits of laughter thinking up messages where Kenny was either begging and pleading for forgiveness, or telling Fliss how stupid she was, we decided to make our message a mixture of the two. Hey, if it did the trick, why not?

"And as my gran always says, in for a penny, in for a pound," Frankie said, looking at the mobile. "OK, here goes. SORRY, FLISS," she typed. "I AM A FOOL. LUV KENNY XX."

Then she pressed the Send button. Done!

The three of us sat in silence for a few seconds. Had we done the right thing? Had Fliss even got her mobile switched on? Maybe she wouldn't get it. Maybe she would get it and ignore it. Maybe – worst of all – she would get it and would try to ring Kenny at home! What if she did that?

Just then, Tiff's phone beeped. A message! She'd written back straight away.

"YES U R" was all it said.

"Yes, you are a fool, Kenny," Frankie grinned. "Ouch. Kenny is still so unforgiven. She is seriously in the bad books!"

"Send another message," I urged. "Same sort of thing. Go on, let's pile on the grovelling."

"I AM A FOOL + A JERK + I'M V V SORRY. KENNY," Frankie typed quickly, and then pressed Send. "This is so great," she chuckled. "Insulting my best friend behind her back – I wish I'd thought of it before!"

Two minutes later, the phone beeped again. "What now?" Rosie asked. "YES, I AGREE," she read. "Ooh, Fliss is playing it very cool, isn't she? We're going to have to call Kenny all the names under the sun before she's forgiven, I reckon."

"I'll get to the point before Tiff's phone runs out of credits," Frankie said, and typed in "LET'S B FRIENDS – PLS?". "Come on, Fliss, give us a break!" she said. "We haven't got all night."

There was a bit of a longer pause between messages this time. Then the phone beeped. "OK," was all the message said.

"Yaaaaaay!" we all cheered. "Result!"

"I take it all back," Frankie said, patting Tiff's phone. "Technology is brilliant. Anything that can make Kenny apologise and Fliss change her mind has to be a complete miracle."

"I'll phone her up," I said happily, grabbing the phone and punching in Fliss's number. "Hiya, Fliss. It's Lyndz. So we're all friends again?"

"Yeah," I heard her say. "Am I still in the Sleepover Club, then?"

"Of course you are!" I told her. "We're all dead pleased to be mates again. Aren't we?" I held up the phone so the others could shout.

"Yeah, me, too," Fliss said. "And by the way, I didn't mean it about being friends with Alana and Katie. They're a bit boring actually." Then she lowered her voice. "Lyndz, I can't believe Kenny said those things, you know. I never thought I'd see the day!"

"No, neither did I," I replied, trying not to giggle. "See you tomorrow, Fliss. Sleepover Club for ever!"

Well, that was that all sorted out brilliantly. There was only one problem left now. Telling Kenny what we'd done. Yikes!

"She's gonna go mental," Rosie said, when we heard the doorbell ring. "She's gonna go totally bonkeroonies at us."

"Yep," said Frankie. "This is not going to be a pretty sight. But we've got to stick together – we did it for the sake of the Sleepover Club and because she was just too pigheaded to say sorry herself. Agreed?"

"Agreed," Rosie and I said, both feeling a bit nervous.

"Right," said Frankie. "Let's face the music!"

I felt even more nervous when I heard Kenny's voice saying hello to Rosie's mum downstairs. This could easily go two ways. Kenny has a wicked sense of humour and could laugh her head off about the whole thing, but she also has a ferocious temper, and could... Well, I didn't want to think about what she could do, really. I had an idea that it would involve lots of pain and bruised shins, anyway.

"You did WHAT?" Kenny yelled when Frankie told her. Her eyes were nearly popping out of her head. "You said WHAT?"

"That you were a moron and a jerk and that you were very sorry," Frankie repeated. "But the good news is, Fliss wants to be in the Sleepover Club again," she added hurriedly. "So, like my gran says, all's well that ends well!"

There was a stunned silence as Kenny digested this information. "Of all the cheek!" she said crossly. "Frankie Thomas, I bet this was your idea, wasn't it?"

"Yep," said Frankie. "Listen, Kenz, I know it was a bit sneaky, but—"

"A bit sneaky?" Kenny snorted, putting her hands on her hips. "A BIT sneaky?"

"... But don't tell me you wouldn't have done the same," Frankie said calmly. "Can you honestly say you wouldn't have done the same?"

Kenny thought about it. She chewed her lip. She frowned. Then a tiny smile appeared on her face. "I'm so gonna get my own back on you, Thomas," she said, half-smiling and half-frowning, wagging a finger at Frankie. "You are so gonna be stitched up!"

"See? I told you she'd see the funny side," said crafty old Frankie. "I knew Kenny had such a good sense of humour, she'd be able to laugh about it."

"I will never live this down," Kenny said

crossly, although the tiny smile was still on her face. "I can't believe Fliss thinks I said all those things to her, that I'm a jerk and a moron and—"

Frankie gave her a hug. "But it's BECAUSE Fliss thinks you said those things that the Sleepover Club is back together again," she said. "So I'm glad you can admit what a jerk you are... Oof! Ow! Geddoff!"

"What did you call me?" Kenny growled, whacking Frankie over the head with one of Rosie's pillows.

"Oof!" squealed Frankie. "I called you... er... a talented, fantastic, gorgeous, wonderful..."

"Keep going!" Kenny ordered.

"... brilliant, amazing, fabulous human being!" yelled Frankie.

"I thought that's what you said," Kenny replied. "Just checking."

The rest of the week was much better and everything went back to normal, thank goodness. I don't think I could have coped with any more arguments! Fliss moved her chair to sit with us again in the classroom, and no one mentioned the words "Poo-Foot" or "jerk" around Fliss or Kenny. Then, before we knew it, it was Friday, which meant sleepover day again!

It was very exciting. We all brought our overnight bags into school with us and then Mr Mackintosh picked us up outside school in his Land Rover as soon as it was half past three. Yay! What an adventure! Sleepovers are always great at our houses, but they're even BETTER when we're having a sleepover somewhere new.

Fliss was almost excited as me. "How are Snowdrop and Jasmine, Mr Mackintosh?" she asked straight away. "How's their mummy? Is she feeling any better?"

Mr Mack smiled at her eager face. "The lambs are doing just fine," he told her. "They're getting bigger and fatter by the day. And the ewe is on the mend, too. Bit wobbly on her legs still, but she's over the worst. The vet's coming to the farm tomorrow to check her over. Hopefully she'll get the all-clear, and she can go back into the fields again, with the lambs."

"Yeahhhh!" we all cheered. That was a good bit of news to start the weekend off.

"And I hear you're going to help bring the cows in to be milked tomorrow morning," Mr Mack said as we headed off towards the farm. "I hope you've got some boots with you – the farm's still as muddy as ever."

"I've got mine," I said, waving a plastic bag in the air.

"Me too," said Rosie.

"Me three," said Frankie.

"And I've got mine, too," said Kenny.

Then the four of us looked at Fliss, who was rummaging in her bag. "Well, check these out!" she said proudly, pulling out a pair of brand-new blue welly boots with glittery sparkles all over them. She waved them in the air triumphantly. "Bring on that mud – I'm ready for it this time!"

Kenny pretended to sigh. "You know what that means, don't you?" she asked.

"What?" Fliss replied.

"I won't be able to call you a certain name any more, will I?" she said sorrowfully.

Fliss grinned. "Exactly!" she said. "You'll never be able to call me that again!"

CHAPTER EIGHT

I suddenly felt a bit shy when we got to the farm. You know me, I'm not usually the shy type at all. But because our sleepovers are nearly always at each other's houses, we can all be really noisy and silly if we want, and it doesn't matter. Being at the farm, I suddenly felt like we were going to have to be on our best behaviour the whole time. And creeping around being quiet and polite is not exactly the Sleepover Club's strong point!

Luckily, Mrs Mack soon made us feel at home. "Come on, girls, I've made a big jug of lemonade for you," she said, bustling us into the kitchen. "And I hope you like strawberry scones too because I've just pulled a whole batch out of the oven, so they should still be warm."

"Yummo," Kenny said at once. "Good call, Mrs M!"

"Now, you don't have to call me Mrs M all evening," she said, with a smile. "That makes me feel very old and boring. Why don't you all call me by my first name – Jackie – instead?"

"Jackie Mack?" Rosie giggled, and then blushed and looked embarrassed. "Sorry – I wasn't being rude, I..."

Mrs Mack – Jackie – waved a hand good-naturedly. "Oh, I've heard them all before," she said. "Jackie Mackie, Mrs Jack... Just call me one of them and I'll know who you're talking to."

Just then, a boy appeared at the kitchen door. Well, I say 'boy' but he was probably about eighteen or so, so a lot older than most of the boys we know. Fliss choked on her scone as soon as she saw him and went bright red. Ahh – did I detect one of Fliss's little crushes in action?

"Is there anything to eat, Mum?" he said, taking his boots off. "I'm starving!"

"Have a scone," Jackie said, passing him one. "Girls, this is my youngest son, Joe. Joe, meet the Sleepover Club. Lyndz, Frankie, Fliss, Rosie and Kenny."

Joe munched his scone and nodded politely at us. Fliss lowered her eyes at once, still bright red in the face. I caught Kenny's eye and we both grinned at each other. Yep – looked like Fliss was smitten again! She didn't even look up until Joe had gone off again, and even then, the tips of her ears still looked a bit pink.

"How are Snowdrop and Jasmine anyway?" Frankie asked after we'd managed to get through the whole plate of scones. "Mr Mack said they'd really grown."

"They have," Jackie said, stacking our plates and clearing them away. "They're in one of the pens. Come on – I'll show you. It's time for their next bottles anyway."

"Can we see the ewe as well?" I asked

excitedly. I'd never seen a sheep up close before, only from a distance. Ever seen *Babe*? It's one of my favourite films, and ever since I first saw it, I've wanted to see a sheep so I could say, "Baa-ram-ewe! Baa-ram-ewe!" to it. Don't tell the others I said that, by the way – they'd laugh their heads off at me.

"Yes, we'll pay her a visit as well," Jackie replied. "She's much better now. Hopefully she can see her two babies tomorrow, if the vet gives her the all-clear."

As we went out, Jackie explained that she'd had to move the lambs from their little home in the kitchen into an empty pig-pen because they kept nibbling at everything. "Doormat, hearth rug – they even started having a go at the chair legs," she sighed. "So I thought, if they're well enough to try and eat chairs, they're well enough to live in a pen for a few days!"

Snowdrop and Jasmine bounced up to the front of the pen as soon as we walked up there, and I couldn't believe my eyes. They looked about twice the size they had been – just after a week!

"They're enormous," Kenny whistled. "Are they really the same puny little things we saw last Saturday?"

"Certainly are," Jackie said, passing Rosie and Fliss a bottle each of warm milk. "Now, you two, stick the teats through the wire and the lambs can have a drink."

As soon as Snowdrop and Jasmine saw the bottles, they got very excited and started bouncing up and down eagerly. Boing! Boing! It looked really funny, as if their little legs had springs on the bottom. Once Rosie and Fliss had pushed the teats through, Snowdrop and Jasmine sucked away hungrily at them, making loud gulping noises.

"This is just like feeding the twins at home," Fliss giggled, meaning her baby brother and sister. "Don't tell Mum I said so, but I think the lambs are even cuter than they are. Maybe we could do a swap, Jackie?"

When the bottles had been emptied and the lambs had nice full tummies, we went along to see the ewe, who was in one of the sheds where it was a bit warmer. She was sitting down when we went in, but when she heard Jackie's voice, she got to her feet slowly and looked around.

"She might be a bit nervous, so don't make any sudden moves or shout," Jackie warned us in a low voice. Then she walked over and gently petted the ewe. "Hello, sweetie, how are you feeling today?"

The ewe didn't have half as much energy as her lambs, that was for sure. I could see what Mr Mack had meant about her being a bit wobbly on her feet. Still, she nibbled gratefully at the pile of leaves and grass Jackie had brought her, and then went back into the far corner of the shed and huddled in a pile of straw.

I bit my lip. It's horrible to see sick animals. I'll never forget when Buster got hit by a car and had to have his leg bandaged up for weeks. It was awful to see him limping around, dragging his sore leg behind him.

"Quick visit to see the ducks next?" Jackie asked, when we'd left the ewe in peace. "There are some new arrivals at the pond now."

"What, you mean ducklings?" Rosie said excitedly. "Oh, cool!"

Splish! Splash! Splosh! Off we went through the mud. "How are you getting on with those wellies, Fliss?" Frankie asked her.

"They're fab," Fliss said happily. "I never thought I would like walking through mud. It's so much fun!"

"It's pretty good mud," Kenny agreed. "Look – you can do mud slides and everything!" And off she skidded to demonstrate.

"Careful!" Jackie said at once. "It gets very slippery by the pond, and I don't want anyone to—"

But before she could finish her sentence, Fliss had copied Kenny and set off on a mega mud slide of her own. "Wheee!" she shrieked breathlessly as she whizzed away.

"Careful!" Jackie called out again. "Don't get too near the p—"

SPLASH!!

Fliss lost her balance and went tumbling through the mud, and then headfirst into the duck pond. Me, Rosie and Frankie watched in horror as she flailed around in the middle, screaming in terror. Fliss is normally a pretty good swimmer but she was so frightened, she'd just gone to pieces. I felt frozen to the spot, as if I was in the middle of a horrible dream.

Jackie rushed over to the pond at once, but Kenny was faster. "Hang on, Fliss!" she yelled and, without a second thought, she waded straight into the water and swam over to Fliss, grabbing her round the waist.

"You're OK, I've got you!" she said calmly. "Now, keep still and hold on tight."

Frankie, Rosie and I watched in amazement as Kenny towed Fliss to the edge and Jackie helped her out. "Oh, you poor thing!" Jackie said, throwing her arms around Fliss who was covered in mud and looked very shocked. "Quick – inside at once. Let's get you warm and dry as quickly as we can. You're all right now, darling. Can someone help Kenny get out, please?"

Frankie reached down to pull Kenny out of the pond and we followed Jackie back inside.

Talk about drama! I couldn't quite believe what had just happened.

"Well done, Kenz," Rosie was saying. "You were awesome."

Kenny hopped up and down to try and get warm. "It's cold in that pond," she said, shivering. "I bet that gave those ducklings a fright. We didn't even see them after all that!"

"It all happened so fast," Frankie said, shaking her head. "One minute everything was normal and the next..."

"Kenny, you were so cool," I said admiringly. "You were brilliant! I hope you're around if that ever happens to me."

Kenny shrugged modestly. "I reckon that lifesaving class was worth doing after all," she said. "Wait till I tell my swimming teacher!"

When we got back in the house, Jackie bustled around with a pile of blankets for Fliss and Kenny. "Get those wet things off at once, wrap these around you and sit in front of the fire until you've warmed up," she ordered them. "I'll be back in a moment with some clean clothes for you."

I had to help Fliss take her clothes off because her hands were shaking so much. "You saved my life, Kenny," she said in a trembly voice. "I can't believe you've just saved my life. I could have drowned in that pond. I'll never be able to thank you enough. Never!"

"That's all right," Kenny said, pulling her jumper over her head. "What are friends for?"

"Yeah, well, I'm just saying, I'm very glad to be your friend, Kenny," Fliss said seriously, wrapping the blankets around her. "I would give you a hug but I think my blankets would fall off if I tried!"

"Don't worry about it," Kenny said with a grin. "Anyway, it was nice of you to let me practise my lifesaving skills on you. Next time, you don't have to throw yourself into a duck pond though. The swimming baths will do!"

Jackie came back in with a pile of clothes. "These are some of Joe's old things," she said. "Not the height of fashion, I'm afraid, but it's all I could find, and they'll keep you warm." She gave Fliss and Kenny a cuddle.

"Now, are you two all right? Would you like to go home? I can phone your mums if you do, I'll quite understand."

"Go home?" Kenny snorted. "No way! I don't want to miss the farm sleepover."

"Neither do I," Fliss said. The colour was starting to come back into her cheeks, and she was looking more like her usual self. She even started to giggle. "Goodness, Jackie, you'll never ask us back here again, will you? We've got mud all over your kitchen floor!"

Jackie smiled at her. "That mud is the least of my worries," she said. "I'm just glad you're all right. Let me make you some hot chocolate while you put those clothes on, and I'll put your muddy things in the washing machine. I think I'll phone your mums anyway, just to explain, and apologise. Oh dear. What a thing to happen!"

"It was my fault for skidding around," Fliss said. "My mum's used to me having accidents anyway."

"No, it was my fault," Kenny said cheerfully. "I was the one who started skidding in the first place. My mum will be all right about it, too. In fact, I think she was half-expecting me to end up in the duck pond when I said we were going to be staying here tonight. Nothing surprises her any more!"

Jackie smiled in relief. "You girls are real troupers," she said. "My heart nearly stopped when you went flying through the mud, Fliss. I thought there would be a lot of tears – but the Sleepover Club is obviously made of tough stuff. Please don't scare me again like that, though. I don't think I'm up to any more dramas tonight!"

Frankie grinned. "Don't worry, Jackie," she said. "We promise we'll try and stay out of trouble – until tomorrow anyway!"

CHAPTER NINE

Once Fliss and Kenny had warmed up in their new clothes – it WAS funny, by the way, to see trendy Fliss wearing Joe's shapeless old dungarees and a faded T-shirt – Jackie said we could watch the chickens going to bed for the night. "But please, please, I'm begging you all, stay AWAY from any muddy bits," she said. "I don't want any more accidents while you're here."

"Don't worry," Fliss said with a shudder. "I've had enough excitement – and mud! – for one day already, thank you very much."

"Maybe a quick dip in the pond before

breakfast tomorrow though," Kenny said thoughtfully. Then she laughed at Jackie's worried face. "JOKING!"

"Look at the chickens going in their hut!" Rosie said, pointing at two fat ones waddling up the ramp. "How do they know it's time for bed?"

"Derrr! Because it's getting DARK, dimbo!" Frankie said sarcastically. "Did you think they had a clock or something?"

It really was sweet to watch the chickens as, one by one, they finished pecking around and wandered up the ramp to roost.

"Good night, chickens," I called. "Sleep tight and see you in the morning."

"Talking of night," Jackie said, looking at her watch. "I think I'd better make you some tea and then show you where you're going to be sleeping. Don't forget, it's an early start in the morning if you want to see the cows coming in."

"How early?" Fliss wanted to know.

"Breakfast about six and then we go out straight after that," Jackie said. "Don't worry if you'd rather sleep in, though..."

"We'll be there!" Kenny said at once. "Sleeping is for wimps. I'd much rather see the cows get milked."

We all agreed on that! There was no way I wanted to miss seeing the cows. So after a slap-up farm tea with piles of food, Jackie showed us where we were going to sleep that night. An enormous loft, right at the top of the house with two big skylight windows in the ceiling – and best of all, a ping-pong table in one corner.

"This used to be the boys' room when they were little," she said. "We put them up here because it's quite soundproof – so you can make as much noise as you want, and you don't have to worry about disturbing us. Give me a shout if you want something to eat or drink, or need anything else, won't you? There are lots of games in the cupboards so just help yourselves. I'll knock on your door at quarter to six tomorrow morning to wake you up, OK?"

As she shut the door and went off downstairs again, we all grinned at each other. Jackie was soooo cool. It was more like staying with a friendly aunt or big sister, rather than someone we'd only just met.

"Who wants a game of ping-pong?" Kenny said at once. "Let's have a tournament – loser has to swim three times round the pond."

"Winner gets to eat all Kenny's strawberry laces," Frankie said, spotting the bag of sweets in Kenny's bag.

"Loser also has to kiss a cow tomorrow," Rosie giggled.

"Or how about they have to kiss JOE?" I said. "What do you think?"

Fliss looked all coy. "He IS nice-looking," she said, putting her head on one side. "Hmmm... maybe I'll have to try and lose."

Frankie snorted. "Try and lose? We've all seen you play before, remember, Fliss," she said. "You won't have to try that hard!"

"Come on, then," Kenny said impatiently, bouncing a ping-pong ball up and down on one of the bats. "Who wants to take me on first?"

I love playing ping-pong. Have you ever noticed that the way people play reflects their personality? Kenny, for example, leaps about all over the place when she's playing. She's the most energetic ping-ponger I've ever seen in my life. Whereas cool, calm Rosie always plays tactically and manages to think about three shots ahead all the time. Frankie likes to do weird and wonderful shots – bouncing the ball off her head or arm or elbow sometimes, and Fliss will often get in a flap and start shrieking with excitement. As for me... well, I suppose my personality shows in that I'm not very competitive. Unlike Kenny, I don't have that killer instinct to win at all costs, and am quite happy to play just for fun. There – that's my ping-pong theory anyway. Which one of us are YOU most like?!

It took us ages to play the whole tournament, but eventually it was just Kenny and Rosie in the final. Me, Fliss and Frankie were getting a bit bored of ping-pong by then, so we decided to liven things up a bit. First we started throwing sweets and toothbrushes and teddy bears to each other across the ping-pong table to distract the players. Then we changed the rules so that the person serving had to spin around three times before they hit the first ball – which made them very dizzy and wobbly each time. Then we put a few obstacles in the middle of the table – like a pile of old boys' annuals and a few socks here and there. Just to make it more of a challenge, you know...

Rosie and Kenny did their best to ignore us and get on with the game. But it became so difficult for them to play that in the end they gave up and decided to call it a draw. "You lot are a nightmare!" Kenny grumbled, opening her bag of strawberry laces and throwing some of them at Frankie's head. "How are professional sportswomen like me and Rosie meant to get anywhere with our ping-pong careers with you amateurs around?"

"They just don't understand the pressure we're under, Kenny," Rosie said solemnly. "They have no idea what it's like to reach the final of the Mackintosh Farm tournament. The hard slog. The stress. The whole country watching your every move..."

"Oh, per-LEASE!" Frankie said. "Stop it already! We'll be getting our violins out in a minute."

There was a gentle tap at the door. "Good night, girls," Jackie said. "Sleep well – see you in the morning."

Kenny looked at her watch. "Yikes, it's ten o'clock," she said. "We'd better get some beauty sleep before tomorrow or we'll scare the cows."

Ten o'clock? The evening had absolutely whizzed by. We all brushed our teeth and got into our sleeping bags.

"What goes 'oom, oom, oom'?" Frankie said sleepily as we lay in the dark.

"I don't know, what does go 'oom, oom, oom'?" we all chorused.

"A cow walking backwards," she sniggered. "Good night, Sleepover Club!"

It seemed like no time at all until Jackie was tapping at the door again. "Quarter to six! Time to shake a leg!" she called brightly.

It was still dark outside and felt like the middle of the night. "Just two more minutes,"

Kenny said sleepily, shutting her eyes again. "Two more minuteszzzzz..."

Rosie blew on her face. "No, Kenz, we're going to see the cows, remember?" she said.

Kenny blinked and then shot upright in her sleeping bag. "Excellent!" she cried, wriggling out and pulling her jeans on over her pyjamas. "How could I have forgotten?"

"What, how could you have forgotten to dress yourself?" I joked. "Pyjamas off first, Kenny. THEN you can put your jeans on."

There's something exciting about getting up extra-early, I think. Usually the only reason I ever do get up that early is when we go on holiday or something special like that. It's quite weird to think about most people in the country still being fast asleep, while you're up and about.

We got dressed as quickly as possible, gobbled down bowls of porridge for breakfast, then put our coats and wellies on. "Everyone ready?" Mr Mackintosh asked us. "Let's go and get those cows, then."

It was such fun! Off we went down the lane in the dark, clapping our hands together to keep them warm. Frankie started singing silly songs like 'O Cow All Ye Faithful' and 'How Much Is That Cow In The Window?'.

Then, once we got in the field, all the cows had to be rounded up. Billy, the black and white collie, raced around barking at them, and Joe and Mr Mack walked around behind them banging sticks against their boots so that the cows would move along towards the gate – and us!

Fliss felt a bit scared to see all the cows lumbering along towards us and shrank back. But the gate was still shut, and we were on the other side of it so we weren't exactly in danger of being trampled! Once all the cows had collected in the corner of the field, Mr Mack squeezed past them to open the gate. "Right, girls, I'll lead the cows. Can you walk with Joe behind them?" he asked. "That way, if they suddenly charge, you won't get squashed." Then he laughed as we all looked a bit nervous. "Only pulling your legs – they won't be charging anywhere, don't worry."

We were just about to set off when one of the cows let out a great bellowing moo and started tossing her head from side to side. She was enormous and looked a bit mad. Mr Mack and Joe exchanged looks. "I think her time's about up," Mr Mack said seriously.

Joe nodded. "Let's try and get her back to the yard before she goes," he said. "I'll give the vet a call. Tell him to come early." Then he patted his pocket. "Blast, I've left my mobile up at the house!"

There was a small cough from behind me. I looked round to see Fliss looking all important and going a bit pink. "You can use mine if you want," she said proudly, handing it over. She looked very pleased with herself as Joe dialled the number and spoke to the vet. "See?" she hissed to us triumphantly. "I told you mobiles are brilliant. You never know when you're going to need one!"

I bit my lip anxiously. I was more interested in the cow. Did Mr Mack and Joe mean what I thought they meant? Was the cow about to... die? I crossed my fingers that she would be all right but she was still mooing like anything and sounded in terrible pain. Poor, poor cow. I really didn't want to see her die. I knew I would cry my eyes out if she did.

I tried not to think about it as we set off. Joe gave us all sticks to whack against our wellies to keep the cows moving. Their hot breath steamed into the cold morning air as they walked along.

"MOOOOO!" groaned the poorly cow, still tossing her head around.

"Is she all right?" I asked Joe anxiously.

He shrugged. "Let's hope so," was all he said. "Put it this way though – I don't think we'll be milking her today."

My heart sank as I suddenly realised the bad side of living on a farm. You would have all these lovely animals living with you, but then you'd have to face up to the fact that they wouldn't be around for ever. I didn't know if I'd ever get used to that.

Even though the others were still singing away as we walked up the last bit of the lane, I went a bit quiet and didn't join in any more. Instead, I crossed my fingers and hoped that the cow was going to be OK. "Please get better," I said under my breath as I heard her give another loud moo. "Please don't die!"

CHAPTER TEN

There was lots of bustling and busying once we got the cows back to the farm. Jackie appeared and led the poorly cow away. Then Joe took us to the milking parlour to show us how the other cows were milked. I noticed Fliss kept very close to him, doing this real girly thing where she kept tilting her head to one side and batting her eyelashes up at him. It was all the rest of us could do to stop bursting into giggles every time she did it.

"I bet you have to be really strong to use all these milking machines, don't you, Joe?" she simpered up at him.

Joe scratched his head awkwardly. "No, not these days," he said, stepping back a little from his adoring fan. "Here, watch. You attach these nozzles to the cow's udder like that, press this button and the machine does all the work for you. Technology, see?"

Fliss gasped as the machine started up with a great hum. "Oh, look!" she squealed, pointing to the tube that led from the rubber nozzles to a tank. "Milk!"

The rest of us giggled. "What were you expecting, Fliss – Ribena?" Kenny said sarcastically.

Joe showed us how they would attach eight cows to machines at once, and then went along the line, turning each machine on. The humming got louder and louder as each machine started, and soon we could hardly hear each other speak. The tank became fuller and fuller as more milk poured into it. It was really exciting!

Once the cows had all been milked, Joe herded them all back into the fields. Then we heard a car pull up round the front of the farmhouse. "Ahh, that'll be Bob," said Mr Mack, sounding relieved. "Excuse me, girls, I've got to get him to that cow before she calves." And off he went.

We all looked at each other, taking in his words. "Before she calves?" I cried, clapping my hands excitedly. "So she's not going to die! She's going to have a baby calf instead!" I felt like a huge load had been lifted from my mind. Phew!

"Awesome!" Kenny breathed. "Do you think they'll let us watch it being born?"

Fliss put her hand over her mouth as if she was going to be sick. "Ugh, I hope not," she said in disgust.

"Come on, let's find Jackie," Frankie said. "I don't want to miss this!"

Just at that moment, Jackie came bustling over to us. "Girls! There you are," she cried. "Sorry to leave you on your own like that. You've picked a very busy morning to be here, haven't you?"

"Can we see the calf being born?" Kenny, Frankie, Rosie and me all said at once.

Jackie chuckled. "Of course you can," she

said. "You'll have to stay out of the way, though, but I'm sure Bob won't mind. Follow me."

Fliss hung back. "Mrs Mack – Jackie – do we... do we all have to watch?" she said. Her face had gone a funny shade of green.

Jackie gave her a hug. "No, lovey, of course not," she said. "You can come and see the baby chicks with me if you're squeamish. One was just hatching a few minutes ago – shall we see if it's born yet?"

"Yes, please," Fliss said firmly. "I can do baby chicks. And I can do baby calves once they're cute and clean. But NOT when they're being born, that's all! Yuck!"

While Fliss went off with Jackie, the rest of us made our way to the cow sheds. "Follow the mooing," Jackie had advised us. It was so loud, there was no question in anyone's mind where the cow and vet were going to be. We crept into the doorway of the shed, just for a peek.

"Hello, girls, come for the show?" Mr Mack said when he saw us. "Don't be scared of all the noise. She'll be all right soon."

The poor cow didn't look remotely 'all right' to me though. She was tossing her head wildly and groaning in pain. And there was the most awful smell in there as well. I bit my lip anxiously as I saw the agony she seemed to be in. "I don't think I can watch this," I whispered to the others suddenly, and went back out into the fresh air. Just that whole animals-in-pain thing again – I can't bear to see it.

Frankie and Rosie weren't in the shed that much longer than me. "It is gross in there," Frankie declared, holding her nose. "Pooo-eee!"

"I think Fliss made the right decision," Rosie agreed. "Shall we go and see some baby chicks instead? It might be a bit easier on the stomach."

Over at the chicken hut, Fliss was sitting down and concentrating very hard on something that was hidden in her lap. It turned out that she was doing a very important job. Jackie told us that a chick had been hatching from its egg but hadn't quite been able to get out all by itself. And because Fliss has such nimble, dainty little fingers, Jackie had asked her if she'd mind carefully picking away bits of shell to help the chick get out – which was what she was doing right now!

"There!" Fliss cried triumphantly, moments later. And sure enough, there in her cupped hands was a tiny, bedraggled-looking yellow chick.

"Well done, Fliss," Jackie said. "I knew I'd picked the right person for the job. Thank you very much. Could you pop the chick on the ground for me so she can dry out in the sun, please?"

"Yes, of course," Fliss said proudly, and gingerly set the chick on the ground. "There you are, gorgeous! You've been born!"

"Who needs a vet when you've got Fliss around?" I joked. "If only calves could be born so easily."

Just as I said that, we heard a shout and Kenny came charging over. "The calf's been born!" she yelled. "And I saw EVERYTHING! It was awesome!"

"Kenny, don't scare my chick," Fliss said protectively, shielding the little thing as

Kenny's great boots clumped across the yard. "You're not the only one to see a new arrival, you know."

Once the calf was all cleaned up, we went to have a peep at her. And oh, she was just *soooo* adorable. She was all wobbly-legged and big-eyed, with the most beautiful long eyelashes. When we saw her cuddling up to her proud mummy, I got a right lump in my throat. Unfortunately, just then, Kenny started telling us all about the birth in full gory detail, which was absolutely gross. Talk about spoil the moment!

"Bob got here in the nick of time, thanks to your mobile phone," Mr Mack said to Fliss with a wink. "It's lucky the Sleepover Club was here, you know, Bob. It all could have gone wrong without them."

Bob the vet had this lovely smile that crinkled at the corners. "Absolutely," he said. "And I hear you've been helping out with those lambs as well. Shall we see if they can go back to their mum now?"

"Ooh, YES!" we all said. In all the excitement of the calf being born, I'd managed to forget about them. There was just so much happening on the farm, it was almost impossible to keep up!

"Come on, then," he said. "Let's have a look at her."

The vet only took a couple of minutes to examine the ewe and nodded at Mr Mack once he'd finished. "She's looking good, John," he smiled. "Right, then, let's see if she remembers those babies of hers. Come on, girl, let's go and find them."

The ewe was looking much stronger this morning – even I could tell that. She blinked in the sunlight once we'd persuaded her to come out of the shed with us. Then we heard a faint bleating from the lambs' pen. Immediately, she pricked up her ears and baa-ed joyfully back at them – and started trotting over to their pen at once!

"Look at her go!" Kenny marvelled. "I never saw a sheep look so happy!"

We followed behind as the ewe bounded across to her lambs, who both started bouncing up and down with excitement. "Oh, look, they're so pleased to see each other!"

I cried, feeling another lump in my throat. Being on the farm was turning out to be very emotional, what with baby calves, baby chicks, Kenny saving Fliss's life and now a mother-and-lambs reunion!

"A ewe never forgets the sound of her lambs' cries," Bob told us. He was smiling, too. "Look at that – what a sight! Isn't nature grand?"

"YES!" we all agreed, without a second thought. Even Fliss!

And on that beeyoootiful note, that's the end of the story. Well, nearly. Some of you who know the Sleepover Club quite well may be thinking, hold on a minute. What about the M&Ms? Did you really let them get away with embarrassing you by reading out the poem to Fliss in front of everyone? Surely you had to get SOME revenge in somewhere?

And for all of you wondering that, don't worry. Of course we got them back! There's no way we'd ever let them get away with making fools of the Sleepover Club like that!

Let me tell you how we did it.

Back at school on Monday morning, we were going round in turn, talking about our weekends as usual. This time, when Mrs Weaver asked if anyone had done anything special, Fliss was the first person to stick her hand up.

"Please, Miss, we had a sleepover on a FARM," she said importantly. "And I helped a chick hatch out of its egg! And we fed the baby lambs with bottles again, and saw the cows being milked and Kenny saved me from drowning in the duck pond – and guess what? We even saw a new-born baby calf, and it was all thanks to me having a mobile phone that the vet could get there in time. Otherwise the cow and calf might have DIED!"

Me and Kenny smirked at each other. Fliss can be just a tad dramatic at times.

"This little calf was so cute," she carried on. "You'll never guess what we decided to call it."

Mrs Weaver was smiling. "Oh, I couldn't possibly guess," she replied. "What did you decide to call it, Felicity?"

119

Now it was Fliss's turn to smile. She beamed right across her face and turned to the M&Ms. "Well, we thought about the cows we already knew," she said in a serious voice. "And we decided to call the calf after them. Which is why we named it... Emily-Emma. Or M&M for short."

The whole class burst into giggles at that. Mrs Weaver looked a bit stern at Fliss's answer. I don't think she'd expected such a rude reply to come from Fliss, who's usually so polite and well-mannered. "I see," Mrs Weaver said dryly. "What a lovely name."

"Yes," Fliss said innocently. "Emily-Emma the cow. We thought it really suited her."

"I do hope you aren't trying to be nasty, Felicity," Mrs Weaver said above the gales of laughter in the classroom. "Because there's one thing I won't tolerate in my class, and that's pupils being nasty to each other."

"Oh, no, Mrs Weaver!" Fliss said, looking shocked. "Not at all!"

"Good," said Mrs Weaver severely, although I couldn't help noticing the tiniest of tiny smirks at the corners of her mouth. It made me think that even SHE thought it was a good name for the calf!

Emily glared at us when Mrs Weaver moved on to the next person. "You are SO not funny, Sleepover Club," she hissed.

"Well, maybe that'll teach you to go snooping round other people's private stuff then," Kenny hissed back, and stuck her tongue out at them. "Serves you right!"

Do you know what? I don't think we'll ever be friends with those M&Ms. But who needs them, anyway? Our time on the farm taught us all something that maybe we'd been taking for granted – that good friends are the most important thing in the world. Even though they might get on your nerves sometimes, falling out with your mates is no fun at all. I'm just glad Kenny and Fliss sorted their differences before the Sleepover Club went to stay on the farm. Imagine if we'd missed out on all those things just because of a silly argument!

Gotta go, anyway. The five of us are meeting up in half an hour to go for a bike ride. Who knows what we're going to get up to next? One thing's for sure – it'll be a whole lot of fun. Long live the Sleepover Club!

40

Sleepover Girls Go Wild!

The Sleepover Club is off to the local wildlife park, Animal World, for the day! Will Frankie enter the Spider House? Will Fliss go anywhere near the snakes? But then Kenny starts teasing Lyndz about what Hissing Horace the python's having for supper. Little does she know what she's started...

Pack up your sleepover kit and let's PIG OUT!

Sleepover Girls in the Gym

Do you wanna be famous? The Sleepover Club does. So they enter a gymnastics competition! The winners get their very own TV show, so it's definitely worth a try. But there's one teensy weensy problem. SAT exams are round the corner, and the girls are in major doom if they don't get down to some serious revision...

Pack up your leotard and roly-poly on over!

Order Form

To order direct from the publishers, just make a list of the titles you want and fill in the form below:

Name ....

Address ....

....

....

Send to: Dept 6, HarperCollins Publishers Ltd, Westerhill Road, Bishopbriggs, Glasgow G64 2QT.

Please enclose a cheque or postal order to the value of the cover price, plus:

UK & BFPO: Add £1.00 for the first book, and 25p per copy for each additional book ordered.

Overseas and Eire: Add £2.95 service charge. Books will be sent by surface mail but quotes for airmail despatch will be given on request.

A 24-hour telephone ordering service is available to holders of Visa, MasterCard, Amex or Switch cards on 0141- 772 2281.

Collins
An *Imprint* of HarperCollins*Publishers*